D0129386

BK 2 TRIPPIN'

THE ACCIDENT

PJ GRAY

SADDLEBACK
EDUCATIONAL PUBLISHING

BK 2 TRIPPIN'

TRIPPIN': BOOK 1

THE ACCIDENT: BOOK 2

THE LAB: BOOK 3

SADDLEBACK
EDUCATIONAL PUBLISHING
www.sdlback.com

ISBN-13: 978-1-62250-932-4
ISBN-10: 1-62250-932-3
eBook: 978-1-63078-053-1

Printed in the U.S.A.
0000/00-00-00

19 18 17 16 15   1 2 3 4 5

AUTHOR ACKNOWLEDGEMENTS

I wish to thank Carol Senderowitz for her friendship and belief in my abilities. Additional thanks and gratitude to my family and friends for their love and support; likewise to the staff at Saddleback Educational Publishing for their generosity, graciousness, and enthusiasm. Most importantly, my heartfelt thanks to Scott Drawe for his love and support.

A FRIEND'S GIFT

Troy left the shelter. He found a job and took classes at night. Troy worked at a meat packing company. He found a cheap place to rent. He bought a used car.

Troy tried to save money, but it was hard. He did all he could to stay off the streets.

Justin left the shelter a year after Troy.

Justin tried to keep a job. But he did not like to work. He lived with his girlfriend. She broke up with him. She wanted him to move out. Justin was going to be back on the streets.

Troy and Justin still talked on the phone. Sometimes they met for dinner. They liked to eat burgers at a diner. The diner's name was the Slop Shop. Troy always paid for their meals.

"I got a call from Cash," Troy said, eating his burger.

"Cash?" Justin asked. "What's up with him?"

Cash was a friend from the shelter. Cash moved to a town called New City. He got a job at an auto parts plant.

"Cash is having a New Year's Eve party," Troy said.

"Cool," Justin said. "I wish I could go."

"Why don't we go?" Troy asked. "I can drive."

"Dude, I wish I could."

"Why not?" Troy asked.

Justin looked at his food. The food that Troy paid for.

"You know I'm broke. I can't help pay for gas or food," Justin said. "I have no job. My girlfriend is going to kick me out. She just took back her cell phone."

"Why not go with me?" Troy asked. "What keeps you here?"

Justin looked down.

"I want you to go with me," Troy said. "This road trip is just one night. I will take care of the gas. And we can crash at Cash's place."

Justin ate the rest of his burger. "Okay," Justin said. "Let's go see Cash and have some fun."

HITTING THE ROAD

It was the last day of the year. It was cold outside and getting colder. Troy drove to Park Street. It was in a bad part of town.

Justin was outside of a house. He was waiting for Troy. Justin had no bag with him.

Troy unlocked the car door. Justin got in. "Are you ready?" Troy asked.

"I've been ready all my life."

They laughed.

Troy stopped to get gas. He bought some coffee for the road. Then they drove out of the city.

"Where does Cash live?" Justin asked.

"He lives about five hours away."

"Do you know the way?" Justin asked.

"Yes," Troy said. "He called me and told me how. I wrote it down."

Troy gave Justin a slip of paper. On it was a map. And some notes. Justin was silent.

"What's up?" Troy asked.

"I have never done this," Justin said.

"Done what?"

"Left the city. I have never left the city."

"For real?" Troy asked.

"No joke. This is my first time out."

"I never knew that," Troy said.

Troy kept driving. They talked about the past. They talked about the shelter. They joked and talked about life.

"Get out the map," Troy said. Troy turned off the freeway. "Cash told me to take this road," Troy said. "It will cut our time."

Justin looked out the window. It was getting dark. The snow began to fall.

Justin only saw open land. Farmland.

NO GOING BACK

"What road is this?" Justin asked.

"This should be Highway 9," Troy said.

It was dark. The snow fell harder. The wind blew stronger.

"Can you see the road?" Justin asked. "Where are we?"

"I can only see snow," Troy said.

"I only see farmland," Justin said. "I don't think people live out here."

Troy gave Justin his cell phone. "Call Cash," Troy said. "His number is on that paper. I want to talk to him."

Justin turned on the inside light. He dialed Cash's number. "It doesn't work," Justin said.

"The phone or his number?" Troy asked.

"I think the phone," Justin said. "I can't get a signal."

Troy put out his hand. "Let me see that," Troy said.

Justin gave him the phone.

Troy tried to dial. "Damn," Troy said. "No signal."

"Troy!" Justin called out. "Look out!"

Troy looked up from the phone. There was a deer in the road.

Troy put his foot on the brake. He turned the steering wheel. The road was icy. The car spun off the road. It hit a big old tree.

Troy woke up. There was no sound. His neck and arm hurt. Troy turned to Justin. Justin was not there.

"Justin?" Troy asked. "Where are you?"

Troy heard a moan from the back seat. Justin had landed there. He was not wearing a seat belt.

"Are you okay?" Troy asked.

"I think so," Justin said. "My foot hurts. It hurts real bad."

"Can you walk on it?" Troy asked.

"Don't know yet."

Troy pushed his door open. He got out of the car. The snow was falling hard. The wind blew.

Troy opened the back door. He sat with Justin. One of the windows was broken. The snow was blowing into the car.

"What are we going to do?" Justin asked.

"I don't know, dude."

"We are going to die out here," Justin said.

"No, we are not," Troy said.

"Yes, we are!"

"Shut up!" Troy yelled. "Shut up and let me think!"

They stopped talking.

"I need to get help," Troy said. "It is our only chance."

"I don't care," Justin said. "I'll be dead when you get back."

"Shut up!" Troy yelled. "Just keep your coat on. Try to stay warm."

"Wait," Justin said. "Look! Out there. Are those lights?"

Troy turned and looked ahead.

"Are those car lights?" Justin asked.

The blowing snow made it hard to see.

"Yes!" Troy said. Troy jumped out of the car. He ran back to the road.

Troy stood in the road. The snow blew harder. He began to wave his arms. The lights came closer. It was a car. And it was their only hope.

LIGHT FROM THE DARK

"Here!" Troy yelled. "We are here! Help us!"

Troy stood in the road. He saw a car coming. He was waving his arms. The sky was black and full of snow. Could the driver see him?

The car slowed. It came to a stop.

Troy ran to the driver's side. "We need your help!" he yelled. "Our car hit a tree. My friend is hurt. We need a doctor."

The driver rolled down his window. It was an old man. An old woman sat next to him.

"Don't hurt us," the driver said. "We have no money."

"Hurt you?" Troy asked. "Didn't you hear me? We need your help!"

"We will drive ahead and get help," the driver said.

"What?" Troy asked. "Drive ahead? We will die out here!"

The man looked at the woman. He turned back to Troy. "Where is your car?" he asked Troy.

"Over there," Troy said. "Off the road."

"Get your friend," the old man said.

Troy got Justin out of the car. Justin put his arm over Troy's shoulder. Justin could not walk on his left foot.

The snow kept blowing. They got into the new car. They sat in the back seat. Troy smiled at Justin.

They were saved.

ROSS AND MARTHA

Troy and Justin sat in the back seat. They waited to talk. They did not know what to say.

"Thank you," Troy said to the driver.

"Yes, thanks a lot," Justin said.

"No problem," said the driver.

The woman did not speak.

"Is there a hospital close by?" Troy asked.

"No," the driver said coldly. "Not near these parts."

The car was silent.

"My name is Troy. This is Justin."

"Hello," the driver said.

The car was silent again.

Justin looked at Troy. "Do you live around here?" Justin asked.

"Yes."

Troy looked at Justin. "Where are we going?" Troy asked the driver.

"My name is Ross," the driver said. "This is my wife, Martha."

The car was silent again.

"Look," Troy said. "Do you have a working cell phone? We can call nine-one-one."

"Don't have a cell phone," Ross said. "Never needed one."

"How about now?" Justin said.

Troy shot him a look. This was not a time for jokes. Justin held his leg in pain.

The back seat was dark. Justin felt the car door next to him. It felt wet on his fingers. Was it blood? It must have been from his leg. Justin wiped his hand on his pants. He did not want to tell Troy.

"Look," Troy said to Ross. "Can you find a truck stop? Anything. We just need a doctor."

Ross looked at Martha. "This snowstorm is bad," Ross said. "We have to get out of it."

"Do you live around here?" Troy asked.

"Yes, we live a mile up the road," Ross said. "We will have to go there. We can call from the house."

The rest of the ride was silent.

HOME SWEET HOME

They made it to Ross and Martha's farmhouse. Troy helped Justin to the front door.

They went inside. Martha turned on a lamp.

Troy and Justin looked around. The living room was old, like Ross and Martha. The chairs looked old. The tables looked old. There was no TV in the room. There was a radio on a table.

"Sit down," Ross said. Ross did not smile. Ross never smiled.

"Thanks," said Troy.

Troy and Justin sat on the sofa. Ross went to the phone on the wall.

"Is it dead?" Martha asked. This was the first time Martha spoke.

"Yes," Ross said.

"What do we do now?" Troy asked.

Ross looked out the window. Nothing but white.

"We can't leave now," Ross said.

Troy looked at Justin's foot and leg. His skin looked blue.

"I think he broke his foot," Troy said to Ross.

Ross looked at Martha. "Martha, get the man some ice."

Martha left.

She came back with an ice pack.

"Now go make some supper," Ross said to Martha.

Martha left the room.

Ross turned on the radio. The report was not good. The storm would last all night.

"You boys better pray," Ross said.

"What do you mean?" Troy asked.

"Pray that we don't lose power."

Ross lit a fire in the fireplace.

SILENT NIGHT

They all sat down at the kitchen table. Martha put food on the table.

"Sorry," she said. "We don't have much right now."

"That's okay," Troy said. "Thank you."

"Thanks," Justin said.

There was some bread. There were some cold cuts. She also gave them some water. That was all.

They began to eat.

"So, do you have any kids?" Justin asked.

"No," Ross said, looking at his food. "No kids."

They stopped talking and kept eating.

"That road you were on," Ross said to Troy. "Why were you there?"

"We left the highway," Troy said. "We were trying a shortcut."

"We want to see a friend," Justin said. "He lives in New City."

"That's about two hours away," Ross said.

"What's around here?" Troy asked.

"Farms," Ross said. "Just farms."

They sat and ate. No one talked. Troy looked down at Justin's leg. There was blood on his pants.

"Are you bleeding?" Troy asked Justin.

Justin's leg was not bleeding.

"No, it is not my blood," Justin said to Troy. Justin looked at Ross. "It was blood from the door. Their car door," Justin said.

"What?" Troy asked.

"Oh, that is from the dog," Martha said. She looked at Ross. Ross was silent. "Yes, the dog," Martha added. "We hit a dog in the road."

"Yes," Ross said.

"Yes, we hit it," Martha said. "It was killed. We put it in our car."

"Where is the dog?" Justin asked.

"We buried it," Ross added. "We were on our way home."

"That's when we saw you," Martha said to Troy.

They heard a bell from the living room. It
came from a big clock.

"It's time for bed," Ross said. He got up
from the table. Martha picked up the
dishes.

"Go to bed now?" Justin asked. "This
early?"

"Early to bed, early to rise," Martha said without a smile.

"We get up early in these parts," Ross said. "Get some sleep. We can get moving early. The storm will be over then."

Martha left the kitchen.

Troy and Justin followed Ross to the living room.

"You can sleep down here," Ross said. "One of you can use the sofa. One of you can take the floor."

"Thank you," Troy said.

Justin said nothing.

Martha came back with some blankets.

"Turn the radio up," Justin said to Troy.

"Will the radio keep you up?" Troy asked Ross.

"Yes," Ross said. "Don't turn it up."

"No problem," Troy said.

Justin looked at Troy.

Ross and Martha began to walk upstairs. "Good night," Ross said without a smile.

"Good night," Troy said. Justin said nothing.

BY THE FIRE

Troy and Justin sat in the living room. They watched the fire in the fireplace.

"What is up with Ross?" Justin said to Troy. "That dude is cold."

"I know," Troy said. "He does not want us here."

"What does he think?" Justin asked. "We are going to kill them?"

"I don't think so."

"Why not?" Justin asked.

"Look over there," Troy said. "I bet that's a gun locker."

Justin saw the gun locker. There was a lock on its door.

"There must be guns in there. He must trust us. Why would he leave us with his guns?"

"Ross? A hunter?" Justin asked. "What do you think he hunts?"

"Ducks? Deer? Who knows?"

"Maybe a dog," Justin said with a smile. "Like the one in their car."

"Not funny," Troy said. "Go to sleep."

"I need a drink, dude," Justin said softly. "Just a beer. Do you think they have any beer?"

"No way," Troy said. "Not these old folks. Go to sleep."

They were both very tired. They fell asleep fast. Troy was on the living room floor. Justin took the sofa.

The snow kept blowing. It kept hitting the windows. Justin woke up first. His foot hurt.

"Are you awake?" Justin asked softly.

"What?" Troy asked as he rubbed his face.

"That blood in the car," Justin said. "On the car door."

"What about it?"

"That dog story," Justin said. "I don't buy it."

"Why not?" Troy asked.

"The car did not smell like a dog."

"Go back to sleep," Troy said.

"I wish we were at Cash's party," Justin said.

"I know. Me too," Troy said. "We will see him soon."

Justin looked across the living room. He saw a photo in a frame. It sat on a small table.

"Troy. Wake up."

"I am trying to sleep," said Troy.

"Over there. That picture on the table," Justin said. "Can you see it?"

Troy stood up and walked to the table. It was an old photo of Ross and Martha. They stood with two little boys.

"It's Ross and Martha," Troy said. "And they are with two boys."

"They don't have kids," Justin said. "Ross said so."

"Maybe it's not their kids."

Troy saw a note next to the picture. He picked it up and read it aloud. *"Don't make a move until we talk. Junior."*

"Junior?" Troy said.

"What does that mean?" Justin asked.

The fire was almost out. There was no more wood in sight.

"Do you see any wood?" Troy asked Justin.

"I don't," Justin said. "But we need more fast. I'm cold."

"What about the basement?" Troy asked.

"Good idea."

"Hang on," Troy said. "I will find some."

ABOUT THE AUTHOR

PJ Gray is a versatile, award-winning freelance writer experienced in short stories, essays, and feature writing. He is a former managing editor for *Pride* magazine, a ghost writer, blogger, researcher, food writer, and cookbook author. He currently resides in Chicago, Illinois. For more information about PJ Gray, go to www.pjgray.com.

He picked up a wood log. Then he went for another. He lifted it. Under it was a foot. He lifted up another. Under it was a leg.

It was a body. A very cold body. The body of a man.

A very dead man.

DOWN ON THE FARM

Troy walked slowly to the kitchen. He did not want to wake Ross and Martha.

He saw a door. Troy felt the door. It was very cold. He knew it was the basement door.

Troy quietly opened the door. He turned on the light. It was not very bright.

There were steps leading down. He slowly walked down the stairs.

The basement smelled bad. Troy looked around. The room was cold and dim. He looked for more firewood.

Troy saw a dark corner. He could not see well. But there was a pile of wood.

"Jackpot!" Troy said.